Don't Be Late

Written by
Akimi Gibson

Illustrated by
Dennis Ziemienski

SCHOLASTIC INC.

New York   Toronto   London   Auckland   Sydney

Copyright © 1994 by Scholastic Inc.
All rights reserved. Published by Scholastic Inc.
Printed in the U.S.A.
ISBN 0-590-27564-X

20   08   1 2/0

Mouse is giving a dance.

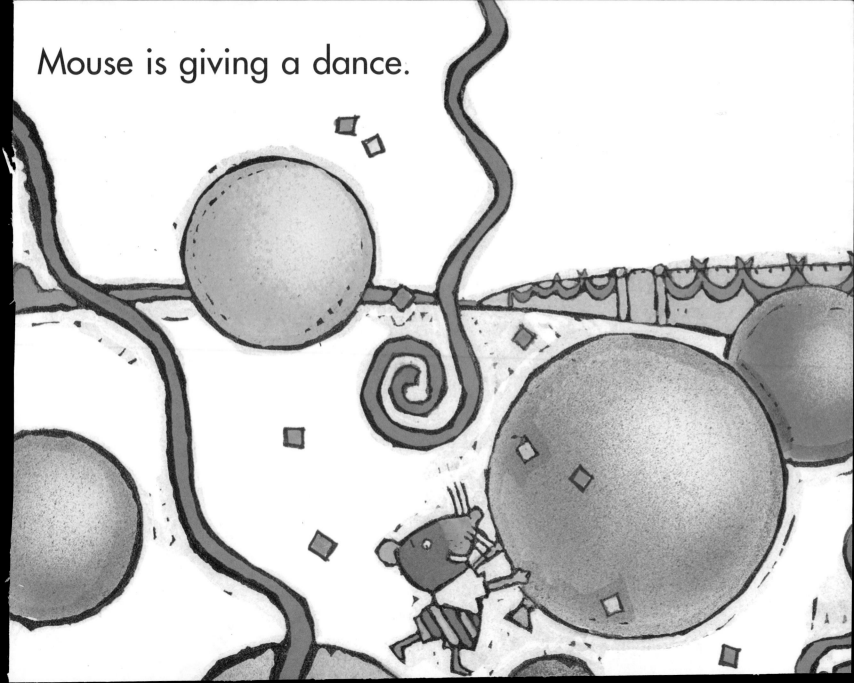

Mouse tells Cat,
"The dance is today in the yard
at ten o'clock.
Don't be late!"

Cat tells Dog,
"The dance is today in the yard
near the clock.
Don't be late!"

Dog tells Hen,
"The dance is today in the yard
around the block.
Don't be late!"

Hen tells Sheep,
"The dance is today in the yard
by the rock.
Don't be late!"

Sheep tells Bull,
"The dance is today in the yard
by the dock.
Don't be late!"

Bull tells Mouse,
"The dance is today in the yard
at ten o'clock.
Don't be late!"

Mouse gave a dance and everyone had a wonderful time.